MAID SERVICE

AN EROTIC ADVENTURE

VICTORIA RUSH

VOLUME 23

JADE'S EROTIC ADVENTURES - BOOK 23

COPYRIGHT

Everybody's an exhibitionist in disguise...

Spying on the neighbors just got a lot more interesting...

Sometimes you need to talk through your problems to lose your inhibitions...

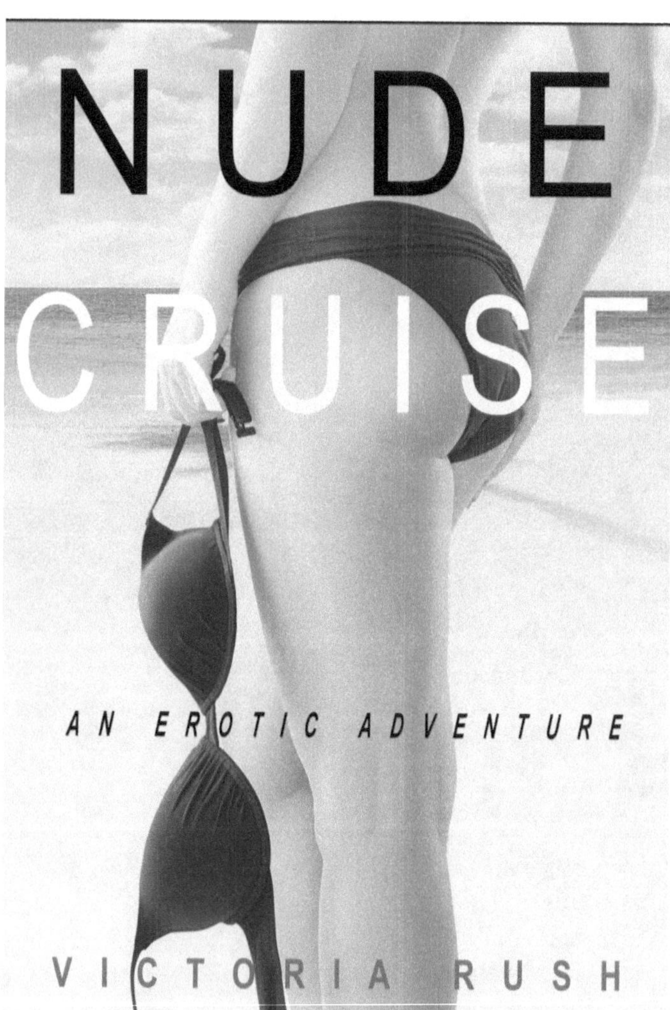

Some people get wet on a cruise for different reasons...

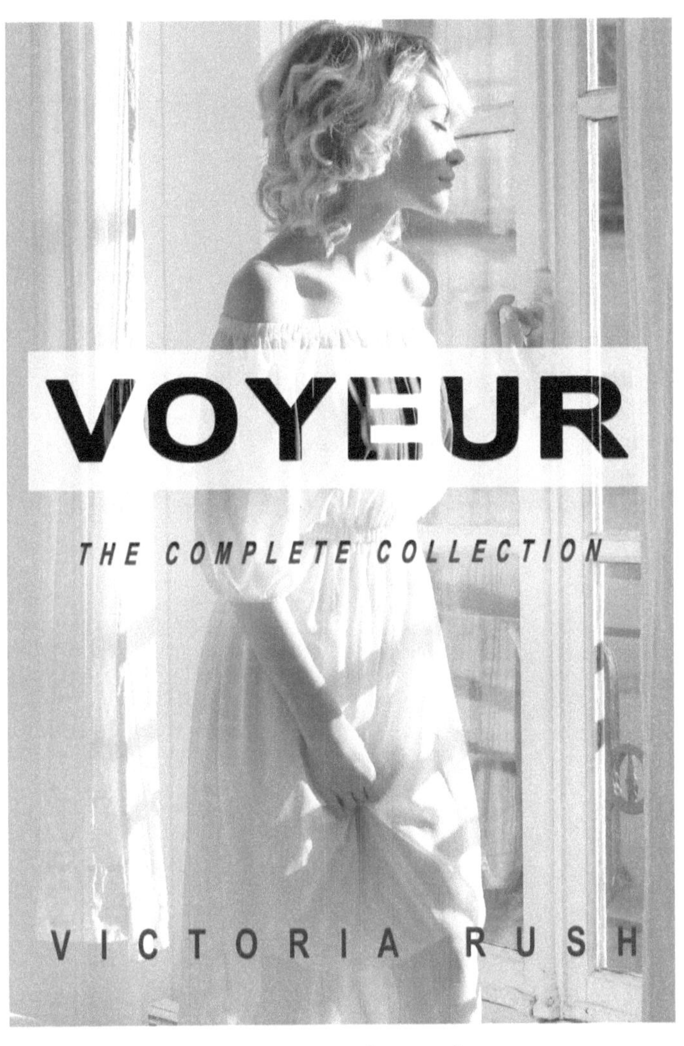

Sometimes it's more fun to watch...

For the uninhibited...

1
———

It had been a long week on the road, and I was beginning to feel a bit antsy. I'd never really enjoyed business travel. The days were usually long, and my nights were often spent preparing for the following day's meetings. Granted, my clients took me out for a nice dinner afterwards, but those too were tiring, as I had to keep my game face on trying to land another hard-fought commission.

Being a freelance graphic designer was a tough gig, and I was always mindful of the need to coddle my buyer while not appearing to oversell my services. The idea of using these getaways for a quick hookup with a new acquaintance was out of the question. Not only was I usually too tired at the end of the day, but I had to keep a professional distance with my business associates.

I'd gotten up early to prepare for an important presentation later in the day, and after rubbing out a quick orgasm and having a shower, I sat down in front of my laptop at the small desk in my hotel room. But after reviewing a few slides of my PowerPoint deck, I paused and stared at the screen. This was the least fun part of my job, and I shifted the cursor over the address bar of my browser, preparing to type in the URL for my favorite lesbian website. I was still buzzing from my morning play time, and my panties were already wet thinking about watching some hot girls tribbing their pussies together. Just as I was about to take off my clothes and make myself more comfortable, I heard a gentle tap on my door.

"Housekeeping," a soft voice called.

Normally I'd ask the maid to return later in the day when I wasn't so busy. But I was caught unprepared and hastily pulled my jeans up before responding.

"Um–just a moment, please," I stammered.

I looked in the mirror at the front of the table and straightened my hair, trying to compose myself.

"Come in," I said, feeling my heartbeat returning to normal.

The maid opened the door and wedged her cart in the entrance, then hesitated when she saw me working at the table. She was younger and prettier than I expected, with dark brown eyes, soft caramel-colored skin, and puffy rosebud lips. I took a quick scan of her curvy figure and sat upright in my chair.

"Don't mind me," I said, feeling my pussy twitch uncon- sciously. "I'm just getting caught up on some work. Do you mind if I finish up while you clean the room?"

"Of course," she said. "I'll just be a few minutes."

She grabbed some fresh linens from her cart and disappeared into the bathroom. As I listened to her hanging up the towels and wiping down the counter, I suddenly remembered that I'd left my used vibrator next to the sink. Horrified, I glanced up and saw her pushing it to the side of the table while she peered up at me in the mirror. I blushed a deep shade of crimson and returned my gaze to my computer, pretending to tap away at the keyboard.

What the fuck, Jade, I muttered to myself, shaking my head in dismay. *Couldn't you have hidden the damn thing before you left the washroom?*

The maid seemed to take longer than usual to wipe down the surface as she rearranged my toiletries into a neat pile at the corner of the sink. I always felt a bit peeved whenever the housekeeping staff moved my personal effects, but today I was more put off than usual. Recognizing more movement out of the corner of my eye, I turned once again to see her leaning over and wiggling her ass as she finished wiping down the countertop.

She was wearing a one-piece black dress with a buttoned-up white collar and a short apron tied around her shapely hips. As she bent over and cleaned the vanity, I watched the muscles in the back of her legs flex while she swayed her hips in little circles. She caught my gaze once again in the bathroom mirror and smiled at me demurely.

Fuck me, I thought. *Are all the maids in this place this hot?*

I returned my attention to my computer and banged away at the keyboard as a jumble of random characters filled my slide. At this point, I had no idea what was appearing on my screen while I fantasied about kneeling between the girl's legs and slurping her pussy from behind. I could feel the wet spot beginning to grow in my panties, and I shifted uncomfortably on my chair, trying to distract attention from my aching clit.

When she emerged from the washroom, I turned toward her and noticed that she'd placed my purple Rabbit vibrator standing up on the side of the counter next to my toothbrush. The simulated penis head and protruding rabbit ears on the shaft stared out at me, mocking me for my absent-minded oversight.

Jesus Christ, I thought. *I wonder what she made of the unusual dildo. Had she even seen one of those things before?*

The thought of her touching my sex toy got me even more worked up as I imagined her pleasuring herself with the multi-functional device. Of course, I couldn't say anything, let alone acknowledge that she'd actually *touched* the object that had throbbed inside my pussy only a few minutes earlier.

As she strode toward my unmade bed, I was tempted to tell her to leave it as it was, since I knew it was hotel policy not to replace the linens until the next guest arrived. There wasn't really any need to make it up, since no one else would be seeing it for the remainder of the day and I'd just be climbing back into it in a matter of hours. But as I watched her glide around the side of the bed, I was so mesmerized watching her body in the mirror, I felt paralyzed.

As she leaned over the edge of the mattress, pulling the sheets toward the headboard, I saw her side profile for the first time. Even though her dress was buttoned all the way up the front of her chest, I could clearly see the outline of her breasts against the background of the stark white linens. Her tits were long and pointed, with wide separation between each peak, like she was wearing an old-fashioned corset underneath her tight uniform. With her light brown hair pulled back in a bun behind her head, I studied every curve and contour of her pretty face. Her cheekbones were high and round like a native American, but her cheeks were carved like a supermodel's. With her golden-brown skin and smoldering eyes, she looked like a cross between Jessica Alba and Jennifer Lopez.

Oh my God, I drooled, staring at her in my mirror. *How*

has this angel not already been swooped up by some handsome billionaire and whisked away to his private enclave? Was this her first week on the job and still too naive to know that with that body and those looks, she could write her own ticket?

As she smoothed down the sheets and wrapped them around the base of the mattress, I leered at her tight ass, fantasizing about all the ways I'd like to fuck her. By now, my panties were so soaked, I'd formed a large wet patch in the crotch of my pants, and I squeezed my thighs together, trying to quiet my raging clit.

When the girl swept around the base of the bed directly behind me, I smelled her perfume, as a light breeze wafted over my shoulders. It smelled sweet and flowery, just like I imagined her to be. I couldn't make out the brand, but I resolved right then and there to go to the nearest department store at my earliest opportunity to find it for myself. Even if it didn't suit me personally, I longed to feel her scent on my body while I fantasied about rubbing our bodies together.

When she shifted over to the other side of the bed to repeat the sequence, I angled my head in the mirror to watch her ass in the reflection of the large picture window overlooking the street. As she leaned over, she swung one of her legs up to support herself while she propped up the pillows in the middle of my oversize bed, and I caught a glimpse of the back of her thighs and a small patch of white cloth between her legs.

Oh, I moaned out loud, imagining what she'd look like completely naked. I wanted this sexy vixen, and I wanted her *now*. But short of jumping on top of her and pinning her to my bed, I was completely at her mercy while I watched her go about her duties. Besides, the door was still ajar, and we'd have no privacy if either one of us had any amorous ideas.

She rearranged the room service menu and placed a fresh bottle of water at the side of the table next to me, then peered up at me in the mirror and smiled.

"Was there anything else you needed, Madam?" she asked.

I paused for a long moment as the words stuck in my throat.

I wanted to tell her how much I wanted to make a mess of her newly remade bed while I wrapped my legs around her and plunged my tongue down her throat, but I shook my head and sighed.

"No," I said. "Thank you for everything. I'm good to go."

She nodded at me, then pushed her housekeeping cart over the threshold, softly closing the door behind her.

Good to go? I thought to myself. *What a lightweight you are, Jade. If you had any guts, you'd have taken her in your arms and kissed her like a proper lady.* After all, she'd given me plenty of clues that she was just as interested in me as I was with her.

As soon as I heard her move her cart to the next room and knock on the adjacent door, I leapt to my feet and grabbed my Rabbit vibrator off the bathroom countertop. Then I tore off my clothes and kneeled on my bed, facing the desk mirror. As I plunged the phallus deep into my dripping pussy and turned the setting to max, I dreamed it was the pretty maid who was staring back at me.

I still have three days to get you into my bed, I murmured. *One way or the other, I'll have you before this week is over.*

2

———

It had been a long week on the road, and I was beginning to feel a bit antsy. I'd never really enjoyed business travel. The days were usually long, and my nights were often spent preparing for the following day's meetings. Granted, my clients took me out for a nice dinner afterwards, but those too were tiring, as I had to keep my game face on trying to land another hard-fought commission.

Being a freelance graphic designer was a tough gig, and I was always mindful of the need to coddle my buyer while not appearing to oversell my services. The idea of using these getaways for a quick hookup with a new acquaintance was out of the question. Not only was I usually too tired at the end of the day, but I had to keep a professional distance with my business associates.

I'd gotten up early to prepare for an important presentation later in the day, and after rubbing out a quick orgasm and having a shower, I sat down in front of my laptop at the small desk in my hotel room. But after reviewing a few slides of my PowerPoint deck, I paused and stared at the screen. This was the least fun part of my job, and I shifted the cursor over the address bar of my browser, preparing to type in the URL for my favorite lesbian website. I was still buzzing from my morning play time, and my panties were already wet thinking about watching some hot girls tribbing their pussies together. Just as I was about to take off my clothes and make myself more comfortable, I heard a gentle tap on my door.

"Housekeeping," a soft voice called.

Normally I'd ask the maid to return later in the day when I wasn't so busy. But I was caught unprepared and hastily pulled my jeans up before responding.

"Um–just a moment, please," I stammered.

I looked in the mirror at the front of the table and straightened my hair, trying to compose myself.

"Come in," I said, feeling my heartbeat returning to normal.

The maid opened the door and wedged her cart in the entrance, then hesitated when she saw me working at the table. She was younger and prettier than I expected, with dark brown eyes, soft caramel-colored skin, and puffy rosebud lips. I took a quick scan of her curvy figure and sat upright in my chair.

"Don't mind me," I said, feeling my pussy twitch unconsciously. "I'm just getting caught up on some work. Do you mind if I finish up while you clean the room?"

"Of course," she said. "I'll just be a few minutes."

She grabbed some fresh linens from her cart and disappeared into the bathroom. As I listened to her hanging up the towels and wiping down the counter, I suddenly remembered that I'd left my used vibrator next to the sink. Horrified, I glanced up and saw her pushing it to the side of the table while she peered up at me in the mirror. I blushed a deep shade of crimson and returned my gaze to my computer, pretending to tap away at the keyboard.

What the fuck, Jade, I muttered to myself, shaking my head in dismay. *Couldn't you have hidden the damn thing before you left the washroom?*

The maid seemed to take longer than usual to wipe down the surface as she rearranged my toiletries into a neat pile at the corner of the sink. I always felt a bit peeved whenever the housekeeping staff moved my personal effects, but today I was more put off than usual. Recognizing more movement out of the corner of my eye, I turned once again to see her leaning over and wiggling her ass as she finished wiping down the countertop.

She was wearing a one-piece black dress with a buttoned-up white collar and a short apron tied around her shapely hips. As she bent over and cleaned the vanity, I watched the muscles in the back of her legs flex while she swayed her hips in little circles. She caught my gaze once again in the bathroom mirror and smiled at me demurely.

Fuck me, I thought. *Are all the maids in this place this hot?*

I returned my attention to my computer and banged away at the keyboard as a jumble of random characters filled my slide. At this point, I had no idea what was appearing on my screen while I fantasied about kneeling between the girl's legs and slurping her pussy from behind. I could feel the wet spot beginning to grow in my panties, and I shifted uncomfortably on my chair, trying to distract attention from my aching clit.

When she emerged from the washroom, I turned toward her and noticed that she'd placed my purple Rabbit vibrator standing up on the side of the counter next to my toothbrush. The simulated penis head and protruding rabbit ears on the shaft stared out at me, mocking me for my absent-minded oversight.

Jesus Christ, I thought. *I wonder what she made of the unusual dildo. Had she even seen one of those things before?*

The thought of her touching my sex toy got me even more worked up as I imagined her pleasuring herself with the multi-functional device. Of course, I couldn't say anything, let alone acknowledge that she'd actually *touched* the object that had throbbed inside my pussy only a few minutes earlier.

As she strode toward my unmade bed, I was tempted to tell her to leave it as it was, since I knew it was hotel policy not to replace the linens until the next guest arrived. There wasn't really any need to make it up, since no one else would be seeing it for the remainder of the day and I'd just be climbing back into it in a matter of hours. But as I watched her glide around the side of the bed, I was so mesmerized watching her body in the mirror, I felt paralyzed.

As she leaned over the edge of the mattress, pulling the sheets toward the headboard, I saw her side profile for the first time. Even though her dress was buttoned all the way up the front of her chest, I could clearly see the outline of her breasts against the background of the stark white linens. Her tits were long and pointed, with wide separation between each peak, like she was wearing an old-fashioned corset underneath her tight uniform. With her light brown hair pulled back in a bun behind her head, I studied every curve and contour of her pretty face. Her cheekbones were high and round like a native American, but her cheeks were carved like a supermodel's. With her golden-brown skin and smoldering eyes, she looked like a cross between Jessica Alba and Jennifer Lopez.

Oh my God, I drooled, staring at her in my mirror. *How

has this angel not already been swooped up by some handsome billionaire and whisked away to his private enclave? Was this her first week on the job and still too naive to know that with that body and those looks, she could write her own ticket?

As she smoothed down the sheets and wrapped them around the base of the mattress, I leered at her tight ass, fantasizing about all the ways I'd like to fuck her. By now, my panties were so soaked, I'd formed a large wet patch in the crotch of my pants, and I squeezed my thighs together, trying to quiet my raging clit.

When the girl swept around the base of the bed directly behind me, I smelled her perfume, as a light breeze wafted over my shoulders. It smelled sweet and flowery, just like I imagined her to be. I couldn't make out the brand, but I resolved right then and there to go to the nearest department store at my earliest opportunity to find it for myself. Even if it didn't suit me personally, I longed to feel her scent on my body while I fantasied about rubbing our bodies together.

When she shifted over to the other side of the bed to repeat the sequence, I angled my head in the mirror to watch her ass in the reflection of the large picture window overlooking the street. As she leaned over, she swung one of her legs up to support herself while she propped up the pillows in the middle of my oversize bed, and I caught a glimpse of the back of her thighs and a small patch of white cloth between her legs.

Oh, I moaned out loud, imagining what she'd look like completely naked. I wanted this sexy vixen, and I wanted her *now*. But short of jumping on top of her and pinning her to my bed, I was completely at her mercy while I watched her go about her duties. Besides, the door was still ajar, and we'd have no privacy if either one of us had any amorous ideas.

She rearranged the room service menu and placed a fresh bottle of water at the side of the table next to me, then peered up at me in the mirror and smiled.

"Was there anything else you needed, Madam?" she asked.

I paused for a long moment as the words stuck in my throat.

I wanted to tell her how much I wanted to make a mess of her newly remade bed while I wrapped my legs around her and plunged my tongue down her throat, but I shook my head and sighed.

"No," I said. "Thank you for everything. I'm good to go."

She nodded at me, then pushed her housekeeping cart over the threshold, softly closing the door behind her.

Good to go? I thought to myself. *What a lightweight you are, Jade. If you had any guts, you'd have taken her in your arms and kissed her like a proper lady.* After all, she'd given me plenty of clues that she was just as interested in me as I was with her.

As soon as I heard her move her cart to the next room and knock on the adjacent door, I leapt to my feet and grabbed my Rabbit vibrator off the bathroom countertop. Then I tore off my clothes and kneeled on my bed, facing the desk mirror. As I plunged the phallus deep into my dripping pussy and turned the setting to max, I dreamed it was the pretty maid who was staring back at me.

I still have three days to get you into my bed, I murmured. *One way or the other, I'll have you before this week is over.*

3

***

I was so fixated fantasizing about the pretty maid for the rest of the morning, I was late for my scheduled meeting with my client. When I got to the office, I could barely concentrate on my presentation, flashing back and forth between her exquisite ass and her Gina Lollobrigida tits. Everybody else in my sphere of influence suddenly seemed so dull and boring. When my buyer invited me for dinner that evening, I reluctantly agreed, knowing I'd have an even harder time concentrating as I dreamt about slipping back under my covers, smelling her intoxicating scent.

When I returned to my hotel room, I lifted the pillow to my face and inhaled her heavenly aroma. For a moment, I contemplated rubbing out another quick one, but I only had a half hour to change my clothes and freshen up. As I leaned over the sink to reapply my mascara and straighten my lipstick, I glanced at my Rabbit vibrator still lying on the counter. Thinking back to how the maid had nonchalantly picked it up and placed it upright next to the sink made my pussy flutter in unconscious spasms.

Fuck it, I huffed, grabbing the dildo and pulling my panties down below my knees. I've still got a few minutes, and nobody will be any the wiser if I have a little fun before heading out to another boring client dinner.

Just as I was about to thrust the oscillating tip into my sopping tunnel, I heard another soft tap on my door.

"Turndown service," a familiar voice called.

Holy shit! I gushed. *Could it be the same girl? How could I be this lucky to see her again so soon?*

"Come in," I said, thrusting my vibrator into the side pocket of the hotel robe hanging on the back of the bathroom door.

When the girl opened the door and saw me in the bathroom, I peered back at her and smiled.

"I'm just getting ready to go out," I said. "Feel free to do your thing while I finish up."

"No worries," the maid said, leaving her cart outside the door and walking toward the center of my room.

I'd always wondered what maids did during turndown service, since I'd been away from my room or too busy to be bothered when they called. But this time, I was intrigued for a number of reasons, and after composing myself in the mirror, I walked out into the room pretending to collect my things.

"I always seem to be getting in your way," I said, watching her collect the throw cushions at my headboard and neatly arranging them on the bench at the base of the bed.

"Not at all," the girl said, laying my pillows down flat on the mattress.

As she worked quietly, I peered at her gorgeous ass, perfectly framed by the white apron tied around her waist.

"I always *wondered* what you guys did during turndown service," I said, looking for an excuse to keep watching her.

She turned her head and caught me staring at her skirt.

"It's mostly just getting the bed ready for you to turn into later this evening," she smiled. "And straightening up a few things like the breakfast menu and the minibar."

I smiled, imagining she was turning *me* over instead, while she ran her hands all over my body.

"I thought it might be something a little more exotic," I mused.

"Oh?" she said. "Was there something else you wanted?"

"Um..." I hesitated for a long moment. Then I chickened out and shook my head.

"No," I said, watching her fold the sheets down into a neat triangle at the side of the bed. "You're doing everything perfectly."

"Thank you," the girl nodded, peering up at me. "I'm still kind of new to this, so any suggestions are most welcome."

"I bet you find some rooms are a little more–*unkempt*–than others," I said, reflecting back on how she'd stumbled upon my vibrator resting on the bathroom counter earlier in the day.

"Some guests are a little neater than others, to be sure," she said, taking a little extra time to plump the pillows at the head of the bed.

"But yours is easier than most," she smiled, lowering her gaze to the cleavage showing in my partially unbuttoned silk blouse.

"Do people sometimes leave things behind?" I said, hoping to steer the conversation in a new direction.

"Oh yes," she said. "Everything you can imagine. Laptops, belts, pieces of clothing–"

"And *other* personal effects?" I smiled.

"Sometimes," she blushed. "But we store everything in the lost and found in case customers want to reclaim them."

"And if they don't?" I said. "Do the housekeeping staff get to keep them as the spoils of their work?"

She placed the breakfast menu on my side table with a fresh bottle of water.

"Not usually. The hotel tries to contact them, and if we don't hear back after a certain period of time, we usually throw it out."

"That must be frustrating," I said. "I once accidentally left an expensive coat in an overhead storage bin on an airplane and never had it returned."

"They couldn't find it?" the girl enquired.

"Apparently not," I said. "I always wondered if whoever cleans the plane simply didn't report it and kept it for themselves."

"That must have been infuriating," the maid said, heading toward the bathroom to check on my supplies.

"Not so much infuriating as embarrassing," I said. "It was the *personal* effects I left in my pocket that bothered me the most."

"Yes, I can imagine," she said, returning to the side of my bed carrying my robe and a pair of terrycloth slippers. "Was it something valuable?"

"Not in monetary terms," I said, widening my eyes as she laid the robe on the edge of the mattress and placed the slippers at the side of the bed. "Just little trinkets I carry with me to keep me amused on long flights."

She felt the lump in the pocket of my robe and reached in to extract my vibrator.

"Like *this* one?" she smiled, placing it upright on the night table beside the bed. "I don't think you'll want this falling into the wrong hands."

"It depends *whose* hands it is," I smiled at her with a raised eyebrow.

The girl paused for a long moment, as we ran our eyes over one another's bodies.

"Do you mind if I ask how it works?" she asked. "I've never seen anything quite like it before."

"*Oh my God*," I said. "You haven't seen the famous Sex in the City episode where Miranda introduces her newfound sex toy to her best friends?"

"No..."

"*Come*," I said excitedly. "Scooch down next to me while I show you what this amazing device can do."

I sat down on the edge of the bed and held out my hand, pulling her down next to me. Then I grabbed the dildo off the nightstand and tapped a button on the base of the unit. I handed the shaking device to the girl, and she wrapped her hand around the shaft.

"Okay..." she said, shaking her head. "That's not so different from most vibrators."

So she has used vibrators before, I said to myself.

"That's only one of *many* ways it can stimulate you," I smiled.

I tapped another button and suddenly the chrome beads embedded inside the translucent shaft began rotating in circles.

The girl's eyes widened as she felt the beads rubbing against her palm, and she took her hand away to inspect the whirring object.

"And get *this*," I said, pressing a knob at the base of the unit.

Suddenly, the head of the penis-shaped phallus began twisting from side-to-side like a possessed wobble-head doll.

"*Holy crap*," the girl said, shifting her weight unsteadily on the bed.

"You've never had your G-spot stimulated in quite the same way until you've tried this baby," I smirked.

"Is *this* the thing you left in your coat pocket on the airplane?" she gasped.

"No, I've got a smaller and quieter device I use to keep myself amused on airplanes. Maybe I'll show you that another day. But there's one *other* feature I wanted to show you on this special toy."

I tapped another button on the base of the unit and suddenly the silicone rabbit ears extending from the side of the shaft began fluttering rapidly.

"These little fingers stimulate your clitoris while all that other action is going on inside."

"No *way*," the girl said, holding her fingers over the flapping ears.

"Do you want to give it a try?" I smiled.

"Right *here*?!" she said. "What about the other guests–"

"It won't take long, *believe* me," I said, squeezing her thigh gently. "With this multi-talented toy, you'll be satisfied in a matter of seconds."

"I don't know..." the girl hesitated, peering toward the closed door. "I don't want to get into any trouble..."

"I won't tell if you don't," I said, thrilled that she was showing newfound interest in my toy. "Here–why don't *I* show you first?"

I pulled off my clothes and threw them on the adjacent bed, then kicked off my heels and sat back against the headboard, spreading my legs.

"Oh my God..." the girl panted, peering down at my glistening labia.

Maybe this business trip isn't going to be quite so boring after all, I smiled to myself.

4

―――――――

"Watch and enjoy, sweetheart," I said, pointing the tip of the rotating dildo toward my opening. "*Mmm*," I moaned as it sank deeper into my tunnel.

When I'd pressed the vibrator as far as I could into my hole, I tapped the button activating the throbbing head and pulled my knees up, rocking my hips in delight. The pretty girl sat frozen on the bed, staring between my legs while I rammed the artificial cock in and out of my slurping pussy.

"You like what you see?" I said, feeling my passion rapidly rising with her watching me only inches away. "Now for the coup de grâce."

I tapped the button to activate the rabbit ears, and the flaps began buzzing against my inflamed gland. I threw my head back against the headboard and pulled the dildo harder against my snatch.

"I'm going to cum, baby," I panted, feeling the wall of pleasure about to overtake me. "Tell me your name."

"Luna," she purred, shifting closer to me on the bed.

"I'm *cumming*, Luna," I groaned as she met my gaze, yawning her mouth open in sympathy with me.

She leaned in and sucked my erect nipples into her mouth, and I whined in ecstasy from the combination of sensations that were attacking my body.

"*Fuck yes!*" I squealed, as my whole body shook like I was having an epileptic seizure. "Suck my tits baby."

I couldn't believe this heavenly angel was actually touching me while I had one of the most powerful orgasms of my life. I hadn't come so hard and so fast in a long time, but there was something incredibly hot about this sweet girl watching me while I pleasured myself.

When I finally stopped shaking, I took the dildo out of my pussy and kissed Luna on the lips. She nibbled my upper lip and I thrust my tongue into her, pulling the back of her head toward me. She moaned in my mouth, and I reached out to grasp her pointy tits, squeezing them firmly.

"Now that we've gotten to know each other a little better, my name's Jade," I smiled, unbuttoning the top of her dress. "Let's get you out of these clothes."

"Okay," she said, peering toward the door uncertainly. "But I can't take too long. My supervisor will be wondering what's holding things up..."

"I won't keep you long," I said. "Maybe we can find some more quiet time later in the evening. Don't you want to give this a try before you go?" I lifted the vibrator off the bed and flipped my legs over the side of the mattress. "Just give me a sec to wash it off first–"

"No," Luna said, pulling the Rabbit out of my hands. "I'll enjoy it more this way. It's already lubed up and ready to go."

She stood up and untied her apron, then pulled her dress down over her hips and placed it neatly on the opposite bed. Then she reached behind her back and unclasped her bra, freeing her unusually shaped tits. She had large brown areolas and thick pointy nipples, giving her boobs in the appearance of butternut squash.

Very tasty butternut squash.

"Oh my God, Luna," I said, shifting over to give her room to sit on the mattress next to me. "Come here so I can suck on those melons. You have the most delicious breasts I've ever seen."

Luna sat down next to me, and I cupped her gourds in my palms, marveling at how buoyant they were given their pointy shape.

"Do you have any idea how beautiful you are?" I said, peering into her eyes.

"My mother tells me every day," she laughed.

"I meant with other *boys and girls* your age. Surely you must notice the way they look at you."

"I guess so," she said. "I always thought it was just because I'm slightly more *curvy* than the other girls."

"You're exceptional in *so* many other ways," I said, turning her chin toward me as I kissed her gently on the lips. "Have you ever been with another lover before?"

"Just some heavy petting with the boys at school. I've never been with another woman like this before..."

I pushed the Rabbit vibrator toward the side of the bed and pinched her nipples gently between my fingers.

"Let me show you what it's like to be touched by a woman. I think you'll find you don't always need *boy* parts to be satisfied."

"But what about the Rabbit toy?" she said, peering at my glistening vibrator lying on the bed.

"There'll be plenty of time for that another time. I'm staying at the hotel for a few more days. Now lie down while I worship your body."

I pulled the corner of the sheets toward the far end of the bed, and Luna lay down flat on the mattress. Then I pulled off her panties and lay next to her while we rubbed our bodies together softly. When she felt my breasts pressing up against her, she moaned softly and I kissed her, rolling my tongue around the inside of her mouth.

"Jade," she purred. "I love the feel of your body next to me. I've wanted you to touch me from the moment I saw you working at the desk."

"Oh *really*?" I said, pulling back in surprise. "You little tease. And here I thought you were ignoring me the whole time."

"How could I ignore you after smelling your scent on the vibrator you left on the counter? And I saw the way you were looking at me–"

"Were you bending over and shaking your ass more than usual to attract my attention?"

"Maybe..." she said, nuzzling her nose into the side of my cheek.

I smiled as I sucked on her puffy lips.

"Do you know what I've been fantasizing about all day long since I saw you?" I said.

"Showing me how to use your special vibrator?" she said.

"No," I purred. "Ever since I saw you leaning over the bathroom counter, I've been dreaming about licking your sweet pussy."

"I was thinking the same thing when I saw you staring at me."

"Did it make you *wet* when you thought about my face between your legs?"

"Mmm-hmm," Luna nodded.

"Spread your legs for me, baby. Let me feel what I've been dreaming about these last few hours."

Luna fanned her legs halfway apart, and I lifted myself up to position myself in her crevasse.

"God," I grunted, kissing my way up the inside of her thighs. "You smell exquisite. What *is* that perfume you're wearing, anyway?"

"Black Opium, by Yves Saint Laurent," she said.

"How perfect," I purred, peering at her dark labia framed by the thick patch of black hair resting on top of her pubis. "Let me smell your flower."

I pulled myself closer to her opening, then breathed in her perfume through my nostrils.

"You could attract any manner of pollinator with that heavenly scent," I said. "I feel lucky to be the first one to kiss you here."

"Yes," Luna panted, lifting her pelvis off the mattress. "Lick my pussy. Taste my nectar."

Normally, I would have teased her a little longer to build up her excitement, but I didn't need any further invitation. I lowered my head and enveloped her glistening jewel in my mouth, feeling her pubic hair brushing against my forehead. She tasted as sweet as honey, and I paused for a long moment, sucking her juices into my mouth. Luna groaned and pressed her mound harder against my face, and I extended my tongue, caressing the top of her lips.

"Yes, Jade," Luca purred. "Suck my rose. Spread me open like a blossoming flower."

"Mmm," I murmured, getting increasingly turned on by the botanic metaphor. I guessed there was a lot more to this intriguing maid than just a pretty face, and I was looking forward to learning about her other interests and passions. But right now, there was only one thing on my mind. Taking her cue, I lowered my head and pressed my tongue slowly into her cavity. Luna groaned and placed her hands behind my head, pulling me harder against her vulva.

"*Fuck yes*," she grunted, gripping my hair between her fists. "Fuck my pussy with your tongue, Jade. I want to cum all over your face."

I was taken aback by her sudden raunchy turn, but her dirty language just got me more worked up as I felt my juices making a giant wet spot on the mattress between my legs. I grabbed the side of her thighs and pressed my tongue as deep into her as I could, then swirled it around in circles, tasting her syrup.

As she began to rock her hips against my face and grip my hair ever tighter, my roots started to sting, but I was so turned on by her mounting passion, I paid no attention. As she began to thrash her hips wildly against my face, I ground my own pelvis against the mattress, imagining I was fucking her with my cunny instead of my face.

Suddenly, she arched her hips off the mattress and wailed out loud as I watched her tits shaking like two melons in a hurricane. Her giant areolas stared back at me with their flaring nipples as I sucked her juices out of her twitching pussy. Luna held me tight against her vulva for many long seconds as her body twisted and convulsed against my dripping face. When she finally stopped cumming, she released her grip on my hair and flopped back against the pillows propped up against the headboard.

"Jesus, girl," I said, peering up between her legs. "You don't hold back, do you?"

"I guess I've been saving up imagining what this would feel like," she said. "Sorry if I got a little carried away. Did I hurt you?"

"Only in the best possible way," I smiled. "That might have been the sexiest thing I've ever experienced."

Luna turned her wrist to look at her watch.

"I've got to get back to work before I get into trouble. Will you have some more time for us to get back together between your business meetings?"

"Are you *kidding* me?" I said, feeling my juices dribbling down the inside of my thighs. "Screw my client. *You're* my new project for the rest of the week."

5

I arrived at my dinner appointment twenty minutes late, using the feeble excuse of a family emergency. But my buyer must have wondered just what kind of 'emergency' had put such severe knots in my hair and rumpled my clothing so thoroughly. But I hardly cared, reflecting back on the memory of Luna's hips quivering over my face. For the rest of the dinner, I barely heard a thing he said, as I nibbled on the red peppers in my stir-fry and swirled the red wine around my mouth, remembering her exquisite taste.

When I got back to my hotel room, I propped myself up against the bed's headboard and watched myself in the desk mirror while I fucked myself with my vibrator, imagining her looking back at me. I slept like a baby that night, then got up early to have a long shower in the morning. I wanted to be as fresh as possible when Luna returned later that morning to do my room. I kept myself busy fantasizing about all the things I wanted to do with her as I introduced her to the joys of lesbian lovemaking. But when the tap finally arrived on my door, it was a different-sounding tone that greeted me.

Hiding my vibrator under the pillow fold in the adjacent bedspread, I opened the door to see an older, frumpy-looking maid. I motioned her into my room, then collected my belongings in preparation for heading to the office. But as I watched her go about her duties, I couldn't help asking about Luna.

"What happened to the girl who cleaned my room yesterday?" I asked.

"We're assigned different rooms every day, so she's probably busy cleaning another floor. Was there something special you needed?"

"No," I said, slumping my shoulders. "I just wanted to give her an extra tip for the special housekeeping services she provided yesterday."

"You can leave it in an envelope on your pillow when you check-out of your room. I'll mention it to her, so she remembers to pick it up."

I wasn't sure if she was telling me the full truth, but I was far more concerned that I'd embarrassed Luna or somehow scared her from returning to my room. Had I come on too strong during our first encounter? Had I misread the signals that she seemed just as interested in me as I was with her? Had her manager admonished her for taking too long to finish my room?

For the rest of the day, I had a hard time concentrating on my client presentations, worrying that I'd lost my chance to reconnect with the sweet Latina beauty. I canceled my dinner plans hoping she'd return for my turndown service that evening, while flipping through the channels on my in-room TV to keep myself distracted. When I heard a soft tap on my door, I practically leapt off my bed, feeling my heart racing in excitement. I tiptoed to the door and peered through the peephole. I was delighted to see Luna standing there with another pretty girl about her same age, both dressed in casual clothes.

I swung open the door and peered at her inquisitively.

"I wasn't sure if I was going to see you again," I said, pinching my eyebrows in dismay.

"Sorry," Luna said, turning her head both ways to glance down the empty hallway. "It was my day off today, and I didn't want any of the other hotel staff seeing me entering your room. We're not supposed to mingle with the guests."

"Of course," I said, looking at her pretty companion. "Did you have any special plans? Would you like to go out for some drinks?"

"This is my friend Gabriella," Luna said. "She works with me at the hotel. Do you mind if I bring her along?"

"Of course not," I said, smiling at the other girl. "I just need a moment to freshen up before heading out. Would you like to come in while I get ready?"

"Sure," Luna said.

I stuck my head out the door to make sure it was clear, then I ushered the two girls into my room.

"I was afraid I might have scared you away after we met yesterday. The new maid wasn't entirely sure where you were."

"I'm sorry..." Luna hesitated. "I didn't have your number and I–"

I noticed the girls shifting their weight awkwardly in the narrow walkway next to my bathroom and I motioned them toward the side of my bed.

"Would you like to make yourselves comfortable while I straighten myself up?"

"Yes, thank you."

I went into the washroom to put on some lipstick and leaned over the sink, trying to see their reflection in the mirror. I had no idea why she'd decided to bring a friend, but my pussy twitched wondering if they might be lovers.

"I didn't catch your friend's name," I called from the bathroom.

"Gabriella," Luna said. "We started around the same time."

"At the hotel? What do you do, Gabriella?"

"I'm a waitress in the downstairs restaurant," she replied.

"You're both so pretty," I said. "I can only imagine how many times you get propositioned by lonely middle-aged travelers."

"It's not so bad," Gabriella said. "As long as we keep a healthy distance and don't flirt too much, we manage to stay out of trouble."

I smiled, remembering how easy it was to lure Luna into my bed.

"Have you known each other very long?" I said, fishing for more details about their personal relationship.

"Just a few months," Luna said. "We kind of hit it off right away."

I was intrigued why Luna would bring her friend to our second date, knowing how sexually charged it was likely to be. As I stepped out of the lavatory brushing my hair, I caught them inspecting my Rabbit vibrator as they giggled quietly between them. I guessed that they'd seen it sticking out from under the covers, and Luna must have been describing its various features. When she tried to stuff it back under the pillow, I held up my hand.

"Don't put it away on *my* account," I smiled. "Have you ever seen one of those before, Gabriella?"

"I Googled it after Luna told me about it," she said. "I've just seen what it looks like on their website."

"It's hard to appreciate it from a *picture*," I said, pulling it back out from under the covers and sitting down on the bed next to Gabriella. "Here, why don't you press some of the buttons and see for yourself."

I handed the purple dildo to her, and she fumbled with it awkwardly.

"Press the little button on the left-hand side of the controller," I said.

Gabriella tapped it, and the chrome beads began whirring in circles around the middle of the shaft. She jumped in surprise and looked up at me inquisitively.

"I bet you've never seen a boy's cock do *that* before," I smiled.

"Um, no..." she said, blushing softly.

"Try *this* one," I said, pointing to the button just below it.

When she tapped it, the penis-shaped head of the dildo began twisting like a spinning top and she almost dropped it in her lap.

"I *know*," I nodded. "If only *every* man could be equipped that way."

"What are these strange things on the side?" she said, pointing to the flexible rabbit ears.

"That's what *really* makes this special," I grinned, suspecting that Luna had already described the unique features of my vibrator in meticulous detail. I tapped the button on the bottom of the device, and the rabbit ears began flapping rapidly. "These two little fingers stimulate your clitoris while the rest of the vibrator is turning around inside you."

I peered up at Gabriella, then smiled at Luna.

"But you already *knew* that, didn't you? I'm sure Luna's

already given you a full accounting of its various functions. You didn't just come here for a few *drinks*, did you?"

"Um..." Luna hesitated, peering over at her friend.

"It's okay," I said, taking the vibrator out of her hands and placing it on the nightstand next to my bed. "I'm glad you brought a friend. There's *so* many more ways we can enjoy this together."

I stood up and took off my clothes, throwing the pieces on the bed next to them, then pulled down the covers on the adjacent bed.

"You never know when double beds might come in handy on a business trip," I grinned.

While I stood in front of the two girls completely naked, they ran their eyes over my figure, lingering especially long at my glistening, hairless mound. Then I held out my hand to Gabriella and motioned for her to join me on the opposite bed.

"Come," I said. "Something tells me this isn't the first time you girls have experimented with sex toys. Let me show you how the *three* of us can make this a little more fun."

I lifted Gabriella off the bed, then pulled her turtleneck over her head and slowly unclasped her bra. Her breasts were smaller than Luna's, but rounder and firmer, with pink areolas and small button-shaped nipples. I cupped them gently, then leaned in to give her a wet kiss.

"You're beautiful, Gabriella," I gushed. "I can see why the two of you came together so quickly. I haven't seen such a pretty pair in a long time."

I peered down at her tight jeans, admiring the youthful contour of her hips.

"Do you need help getting out of those pants?"

"Yes please," she said as I watched her nipples contract and harden in excitement.

I reached down and unclasped the button at the top of her waistband, then lowered the zipper and pulled her jeans down to the floor as she kicked them off to the side. Then I kneeled down between her thighs and pulled her panties down to the floor, and she stepped out of them. Her bush was trimmed more neatly than Luna's, with a tawny amber color, and I leaned in to kiss it while I reached around and cupped her buttocks gently. Her ass quivered as I lowered my mouth to her moist slit, and she gasped when I circled her nub with my lips.

"Mmm," I moaned, as she pressed her mound harder into my face.

I peered out of the side of my eyes at Luna still sitting on the edge of the other bed, noticing her hand moving gently in her lap. The thought of her watching me while I ate out her best friend thrilled me, and I began to roll my hips unconsciously as I licked and teased Gabriella's burning clit.

"Uhnn," she grunted, spreading her legs further apart and angling her hips until she was standing directly over top of me. I squeezed her cheeks while her buttocks clenched together, and from the pace of her breathing I knew it wouldn't be long before she reached the peak of her pleasure.

I tilted my head up and watched her little boobs bouncing on her chest as she ran her fingers through my hair. She wasn't as aggressive as Luna had been holding me while I sucked her pussy, and I guessed that she was the submissive one in the relationship.

"Oh *God*," Gabriella suddenly moaned as she slumped over me, jerking her body in spastic movements.

I could tell from the intensity of her rocking motion that

she was cumming on my face, and I held her tightly until she stopped moving. I pulled my head back and peered over at Luna, who had her knees spread wide apart and was rubbing her hand vigorously over a large stain in the crotch of her jeans.

"I think somebody *else* is missing out on all the fun," I said, shifting over and pulling her pants down over her curvy hips.

This time she'd chosen to go pantyless, and I looked up at her with a mischievous smile.

"Were you in a hurry to get started tonight?" I grinned.

"Going bare just reminded me of what it felt like to have you next to me," she smiled. "I didn't want anything else getting in the way."

I pulled her off the bed and ripped off her T-shirt, thrilled to see her oval-shaped melons bouncing freely on her chest.

"*Gawd*, how I've fantasized about these since I last saw you," I panted, pulling her toward me, mashing our bodies together. "But first, I had something different in mind."

I yanked the opposite bedspread all the way down toward the baseboard and instructed the two girls to kneel on the mattress, facing one another.

"I want to watch you enjoy my special vibrator together."

I handed the dildo to Gabriella and smiled.

"Why don't you place the long end inside, then press your bodies together so you can *both* enjoy the vibrating rabbit ears?"

Gabriella looked at Luna, and her friend nodded back at her.

"Knock yourselves out while I make myself more comfortable," I smiled.

I leaned back on my mattress and began circling my clit

while I watched the two girls rubbing their bodies together. Gabriella tapped the buttons on the base of the unit and slowly inserted the oscillating device into her hole. She gasped in surprise at the unusual sensation, and Luna wrapped her arms around her shoulders, pulling their bodies together. As Gabriella began to thrust the humming vibrator in and out of her pussy, Luna pressed her mound against her girlfriend, purring in delight.

"Press the knob on the bottom now," I said to Gabriella, inserting two fingers into my slit.

Gabriella peered over at me, and her eyes widened as she watched me finger-fucking myself with my knees spread wide apart. She reached behind her ass and flexed her finger, and I heard a loud buzzing sound emanating from between their legs. The two girls groaned in pleasure as they felt the rabbit ears flapping against their joined clits, then they pressed their faces together, tonguing each other wildly. The image of the two sexy girls rubbing their bodies together as the big dildo whirled, twisted, and buzzed between both of their legs was surreal.

"*Fuck* yes," I hissed, ramming my fingers harder into my cunt. "Rub your tits and cunnies together while I watch you come."

"Mmm," Luna moaned, placing her hands over Gabriella's buttocks. "Come with me, Gabby," she said. "I can feel the rabbit ears touching both of our clits."

"Yes," Gabby whinnied, reaching around to grab Luna's ass at the same time. "I'm cumming, Lou. Oh *God*, I'm *cumming*!"

The two girls tilted their heads back and wailed in unison as their bodies began to quiver and tremble in simultaneous orgasm. I'd been so focused on watching them rubbing their bodies together that I'd barely paid any attention to what *I* was feeling, but the sight of them cumming together with my favorite vibrator purring between their legs quickly put me over the edge. I lifted my hips off the bed and thrust my fingers deep into my snatch and uttered a deep, guttural moan.

"Fuck *me*," I said, feeling my pussy clamp down hard over my fingers as my body levitated a foot above of the mattress. I held my body in this arched position for many long seconds while the three of us grunted and screamed in simultaneous ecstasy.

Suddenly I remembered where we were, and how thin the walls were between the adjoining rooms.

I wonder if all the other guests are expecting a similar type of turndown service, I smiled, flopping down onto the mattress in exhaustion.

6

———

W hen the girls lay down on the bed after coming down from their tandem orgasm, I nestled in next to them, and we cuddled silently for a few minutes. It felt incredible to have two gorgeous angels lying next to me as we nibbled and caressed each other's bodies, with nobody wanting to acknowledge what had just happened. But as they became progressively more daring in exploring my body, Luna pulled away and peered at her friend.

"I think it's *Jade's* turn now to get a little direct attention, don't you think Gabby?"

Gabriella nodded, and Luna turned her head toward me, lifting the Rabbit vibrator off the bed.

"How can we put this thing to work for all *three* of us?" she said. "We have too many body parts for one device to stimulate us at the same time."

I raised myself up on one arm and pushed the vibrator back down onto the mattress.

"I think each of us have had plenty enough stimulation

from that thing. I'd far rather play with some flesh and blood pretty *girls* than have another cock inside me."

"Mmm," Luna grinned. "What can we do for *you* now that you've given us so much pleasure?"

I peered at Luna's tubular breasts and smiled.

"I've been fantasizing all day about you fucking me with those pretty melons. I want you to diddle me with your special tits."

"Okay," she said, lifting an eyebrow. "But what about Gabby? It seems such a waste for her to just stand by and *watch*."

I peered over at Gabriella and hesitated as I contemplated how to get all three of us involved at the same time. Then a huge grin slowly spread over my face.

"I have an idea," I said. "I'll lie down on the bed while Gabby straddles my face, as you lift up my hips and support me from behind. That way, you both can get a bird's-eye view of the action while I get serviced from both sides."

Luna's eyes opened wide as saucers as she pictured the scene in her mind.

"Holy shit," she said. "That will be so hot. Plus, we can *both* play with your pretty pussy from that position!"

"What are you waiting for?" I said, lying down with my ass pointed toward the headboard. "Come here little girl and sit on my face."

Gabriella got up on her hands and knees and placed her legs on opposite sides of my head facing Luna. As she slowly lowered her dripping pussy onto my face, Luna raised my hips off the bed and pressed her chest into my lower back until my body was perpendicular to the mattress. Then she spread her knees for support and pushed my legs apart. As my feet dangled in the air beside her shoulders, she grabbed one of her tits and pointed her erect teat toward my quivering hole. When I felt her flesh press against my vulva, I grunted into Gabriella's pussy writhing over my face.

"*Uhhn*," I groaned, unable to speak with my mind spinning in pleasure.

When Luna began rubbing her breast up and down my slit, I could hear the soft sloshing sound my pussy made as my labia puckered in and out in involuntary reflex. Although I couldn't see what she was doing with Gabby's ass buried over my face, the thought of them both looking at my upturned pussy drove me wild with pleasure.

Just when I thought it couldn't get any better, Gabby leaned forward and encircled my inflamed bud with her lips, rolling her tongue over my gland while she squeezed my tits. With her head now getting in the way of Luna's titfucking, her friend lowered her face down my perineum and began licking my freshly washed pucker.

I couldn't believe that every part of my body was now being serviced by these two angels, and I grunted in mounting ecstasy as my hips began to shake from my approaching orgasm. When it finally hit me, I growled like a wild animal while Gabriella pressed her pussy hard against my face and moaned along with me as she sucked my inflamed bean like a lollypop. When I felt Luna's tits rubbing against the back of my hips, my juices spurted out of me like a geyser, spraying all over both of the girls' faces.

I came for the longest time as the two girls held my body in this upright position, quivering and spurting while the entire length of my perineum flexed in powerful contractions. I wondered if Luna noticed my rosebud clenching in powerful contractions from her front-row seat immediately above my elevated pelvis. Either way, the thought of my most intimate parts exposed to their direct view as I came mere inches away from both of their faces magnified my arousal as I grunted under the weight of Gabby's trembling hips. When I finally stopped cumming, Luna lowered my hips back down onto the mattress and both girls lay beside me, caressing my drenched tits and abdomen.

"Oh my God," I panted, watching stars floating above my head as my mind spun in a drunken stupor. "That was even hotter than I imagined. I don't think I've come that hard in my entire life."

"We *noticed*," Luna smiled, wiping my juices off her face with the back of her hand. "You really opened the taps unexpectedly on the two of us."

"Sorry. I do that when I'm especially turned on. And I've never been stimulated like that before. That was incredible."

"We enjoyed it just as much as you did," Gabriella said, sucking my nipples softly into her mouth.

"Really?" I said, holding her head gently against my chest. "I couldn't tell with your hips buried on top of my face. Did you cum too? I didn't want to leave you hanging–"

"Oh, I *came* alright. Maybe not with the same degree of fireworks that you did, but when you started squirting all over my face, you opened the taps for me too. I've never been in a threesome before. Thanks for inviting me into your room."

I peered over at Luna and smiled.

"I think we have your friend to thank for that. I'm guessing this isn't the first time the two of you have had girl-on-girl sex before."

"No," Gabriella blushed. "But never quite like this."

"You know," I said, smiling at the two girls, realizing I had a once-in-a-lifetime opportunity. "We don't have a lot of time left before I have to leave town. We should make the best of our remaining time together."

"What else did you have in mind?" Luna said, propping herself up on an elbow.

"Everything we've done so far has been one-on-one, or just two girls enjoying each other's bodies. We still haven't had a chance for all *three* of us to come together yet."

Luna peered up at me and smiled.

"I have to confess that I was touching myself while I rubbed my breasts against your pussy," she said. "I came soon after I saw both of you climaxing."

"That makes me happy," I said, leaning in to kiss her moist lips. "But I was thinking of something even *more* interactive. Something where we all can be joined together at the same time."

The girls peered at me with a confused expression, shaking their heads.

"How is that even *possible*?" Gabriella said, pinching her eyebrows. "With each of us having separate lady parts, how would we be able to touch them together simultaneously?"

"Surely you two have experimented with different types of *scissoring*?" I smiled.

"Yes..." Gabby blushed.

"Have you ever tried it *back-to-back*?" I said.

"How do you mean?" Luna said.

"I mean *ass-to-ass*. Two of us could rub our vulvas together, with the third one lying underneath as we ground our mounds together. I've never actually tried it, but I'm thinking it might work if we position ourselves the right way."

"I'm up for giving it a try," Luna smiled. "But who'll be on top and who'll be on the bottom?"

I looked at Luna and grinned.

"Something tells me you like to be the dominant one," I said. "Besides, I still haven't had quite enough of you. I've been dreaming about cunt-fucking you ever since I laid eyes on you. What do you say, Gabby? Would you like to have two sexy girls rubbing their pussies over top of you while you wrap your legs around our asses?"

"Oh my God," she gushed, turning her head toward Luna. "You weren't kidding when you told me about this crazy woman. I'm almost cumming just *thinking* about it!"

"It's *your* turn to lie down on the bed, girl," I instructed. "Would you like to take the inferior or superior position, Luna?"

Luna paused for a moment as she looked at me, trying to interpret my meaning. Then she nodded her head and smiled.

"I'll face her lower body, while you play with Gabby's tits.

That way, I can watch her pussy twitching when we all come together."

"Works for me," I smiled, lifting my knee and placing my legs on opposite sides of Gabriella's hips.

Luna turned around and did the same thing, but with her head pointed toward Gabby's feet. We shifted our weight slightly backwards and when our asses touched, we arched our backs, angling our vulvas toward one another. When we felt our clits touch, each of us groaned.

"*Fuck*, yes," Luna hissed. "I want to feel you spray all over my ass when you come this time, Jade."

"My pleasure, hun," I said, peering into Gabby's eyes. "What do you say, Gab, are you ready to give this a try?"

"Damn *straight*," she said, pulling my head down and thrusting her tongue deep into my mouth.

As I swiveled my hips against Luna's ass and dripping pussy, I mashed my tits against Gabriella's chest, listening to her groan in my mouth. She tilted her hips and lifted her buttocks off the bed as I felt her grinding her mound against mine.

"That's it, baby," I purred. "Fuck my pussy while Luna tribs my ass. I'm going to spray all over your pretty cunny when I come."

"Mmm," Gabby moaned as I kissed her wildly.

The three of us were twisting our hips and grinding our pussies together, trying to find the right position where each of our clits received the ideal stimulation. I could feel Luna's labia intermingling with my own, and our pussies made nasty slurping noises as our asses smacked together. While our mutual passion escalated into a noisy cacophony of grunts and moans, Gabriella wrapped her arms and legs around my back and pressed her chest harder against my tits as she began to make funny squealing noises.

I knew she was close to cumming and as my *own* pleasure began to crest, I could feel it rushing toward me like a freight train. When the orgasm suddenly washed over me, the walls of my pussy suddenly clamped down hard and I began gushing all over Luna's bare ass and Gabby's pussy. Luna's buttocks began quaking next to mine as she howled in delight watching her girlfriend's vulva slapping open and shut in the throes of her own powerful climax. All three of us were climaxing now as we ground our pussies together in glorious union, grasping and clutching each other wildly. As we quivered, dripped, and squirted in mutual ecstasy for what seemed like an eternity, I suddenly became aware of how soaked the sheets had become.

It's going to be one hell of a clean-up operation for the next housekeeper, I smiled. *But no matter—with the generous tip I plan to leave on my pillow when I check out, something tells me she won't mind.*

Everybody's an exhibitionist in disguise...

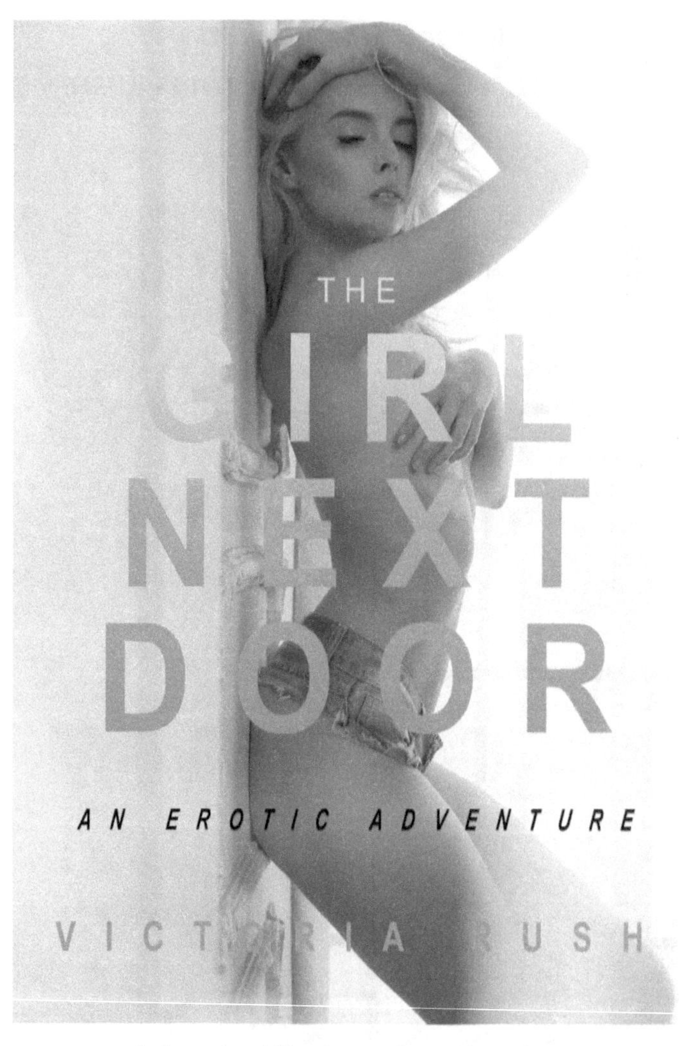

Spying on the neighbors just got a lot more interesting...

Sometimes you need to talk through your problems to lose your inhibitions...

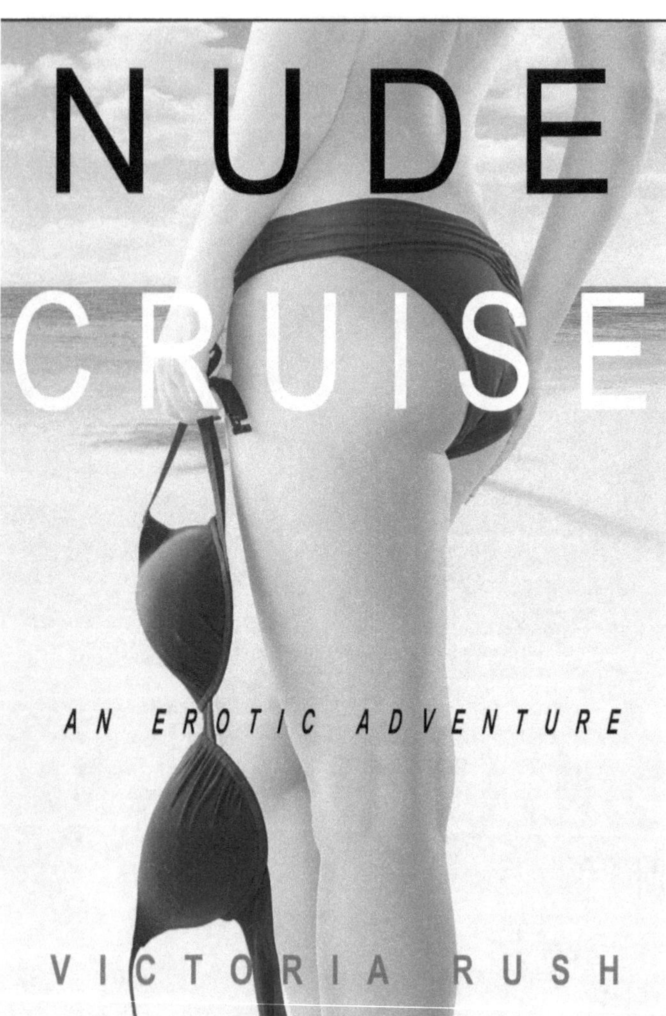

Some people get wet on a cruise for different reasons...

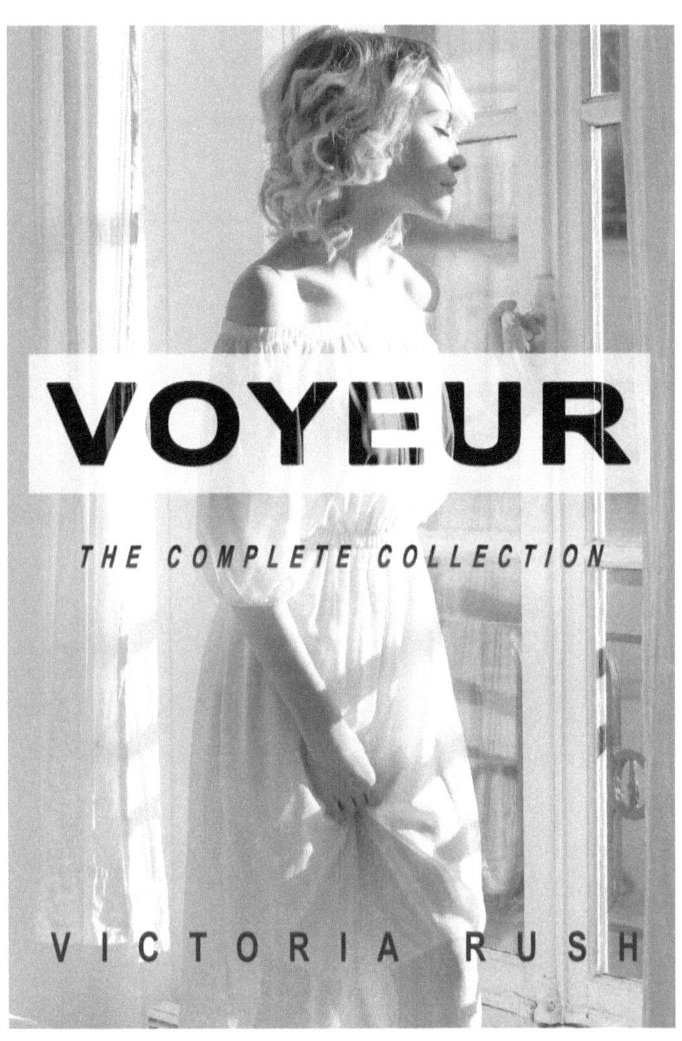

Sometimes it's more fun to watch...

THE DINNER PARTY - PREVIEW
FINGER FOOD

S ometime later, I heard a soft tap on my bedroom door. Not wanting to remove myself just yet from my cocoon of luxury, I called out to answer.

"Yes?"

"It's time for your massage," a woman's voice replied.

"Just one minute please."

I reluctantly stepped out of the bath and quickly toweled myself dry. I wrapped a large bath sheet around me, re-donned my mask, then opened the bedroom door.

A petite young Asian girl greeted me, wearing a kimono similar to mine and a crimson masquerade mask.

Apparently not everybody who works here always walks around stark naked.

The girl was utterly breathtaking. Long jet-black hair cascaded over high cheekbones past pouty lips, her delicate collarbones peeking from the top of her kimono. I could see her breasts and hips outlined by the tightly-wrapped kimono and suddenly wished that she too had come to my boudoir naked.

"My name is Jasmine," she said. "I'm your personal

masseuse and esthetician. Are you ready for your final preparation?

Just the thought of this beauty laying her tender hands on me sent a shiver down my spine.

"Definitely. Please come in. How would you like me to prepare?"

"Come with me, please."

Jasmine led me into the bathroom, where she nonchalantly removed her kimono and hung it behind the bathroom door.

Oh my God.

I didn't think anyone in this place could get more beautiful or sensuous. Jasmine had perfectly shaped B-cup breasts with a thin indentation running down the center of her perfectly toned stomach. Like everyone else in this place, her pubis was utterly bald and flawless. She barely looked eighteen and I was just about to ask her age, but she spoke first.

"If you'd like to remove your towel and lay face down on the table, we can get started. May I call you Jade?"

There was something about her confident manner and tone that belied her youthful appearance. I had no inhibitions whatsoever about displaying myself unclothed to this stranger.

"Yes, thank you, Jasmine." I unhooked my bath sheet and threw it against the side of the tub.

"Would you like me to drape your backside?" Jasmine asked.

"That won't be necessary," I quickly answered.

Jasmine walked over to the vanity counter and picked up two small bottles of oil resting under an orange radiant lamp. She brought them back to the massage table, opened one, and poured the oil into one cupped hand then rubbed her hands together. The scent of lavender wafted toward my nose.

I closed my eyes in anticipation of her touch. I'd had massages before, but nothing as sensuous and stimulating as this. When her hands touched the small of my back, I jerked reflexively from the sexual tension. My heart was beating a hundred miles an hour as I felt the blood coursing through my veins.

Jasmine must have sensed my nervous tension and began pressing her fingers more firmly into my back as she moved them slowly up each side of my spine. The warm oil allowed her hands to glide effortlessly across my skin. She used every surface of her hands to massage my muscles, expertly kneading my skin with her fingers and palm.

I began to relax as my muscles softened and surrendered to her touch. She sensuously massaged every part of my back, shoulders, and neck, applying just the right amount of pressure. Periodically, she would pour more warm oil on my lower back, dipping her hands in it to replenish the silky lubrication against my pliant skin.

Just as the sexual tension began to subside from the utter relaxation of the massage, Jasmine moved her hands down to my buttocks and began to caress them in soft circular motions. My glutes contracted involuntarily and I unconsciously pressed my mound into the firm padding of the table. Suddenly I was quickly reminded that a gorgeous young woman was caressing my naked body. She cupped each buttock between her hands as she massaged my ass tantalizingly, her little finger sliding slowly into the cleft just above my anus.

Periodically, I'd partially open one of my eyes with my head turned in her direction to look at her gorgeous body. My head was at the same level as her midsection, and my mouth watered as I watched her stomach muscles flex and her hips undulate with each movement of her hands. At times her pussy was almost right beside me and I wanted to reach out and run my own fingers up her soft legs.

I was in total heaven and getting wetter by the moment. Just when I thought I couldn't stand it anymore, she suddenly moved her hands down to my feet and began massaging her thumbs into my soles.

I'd always loved having my feet massaged, but nobody did it like Jasmine. She cradled my foot and used every part of her hands to massage and knead every surface from my heel to my toes. I didn't want her to stop, but there were other parts of my body that were screaming for attention.

As if reading my thoughts, she began moving her hands up toward my calf, using her thumbs to spread the muscle apart. She lingered almost as long on my calf as she had on my foot, rolling the ball of my calf between both of her hands, sliding her slick hands up and down erotically. I couldn't help imagining how she might use those same hands to massage a man's erect cock in a similar manner. My mind wandered again to what pleasures lay in wait for me over dinner.

After shifting her hands to my right leg and giving my other foot and calf similar attention, she placed each hand just behind my knees and began to slowly move them up towards my buttocks. Her thumbs pressed against my inner thighs as she glided tantalizingly close to my apex.

I rolled my legs outward in an invitation to move closer. My legs were parted enough that I was sure she could see my vulva from her vantage point behind me. In my highly aroused state, my lips were engorged and spread apart, revealing my moist and quivering opening.

But as much as I desperately wanted her to, Jasmine

never touched me there. She repeatedly slid her hands right up to the edge of my slit, pressing and rotating her thumbs on the fleshy meat of my upper thighs just below my aching pussy. I suppose this was part of her master plan—to tease me mercilessly and inflame my passions so I'd be ready for just about anything at the main event.

It was certainly working. After thirty minutes of Jasmine's ministrations, I was grinding my pussy into the table trying desperately to give my clit some needed direct stimulation.

Just when I thought I couldn't be teased any more tantalizingly, Jasmine opened one of the bottles of warm oil and poured it directly into the crack of my ass. She paused as the fluid flowed down and directly over my parted lips. I almost came from the gentle movement of the warm liquid as it trickled across the folds of my labia, channeled toward the junction where they joined together at my clit. I shuddered in pleasure at the feeling, even if it was only the subtlest of touch.

Jasmine suddenly interrupted my thoughts.

"Would you like to turn over now?"

It was the first time she had spoken directly to me since the massage started, and it surprised me in my catatonic, pre-orgasmic state. I practically flipped over like a fish out of water and spread my legs expectantly. Finally, I'd get some relief. Surely, she couldn't leave me hanging like this.

"It's time for your final grooming," she said. "I'll need you to part your legs a bit further to provide full access."

Grooming? I knew this was part of the process, but somehow it didn't seem fair to transition at this precise moment. At least I'd be able to stay on the comfortable massage table instead of the clinical vinyl chairs used by my regular esthetician.

Jasmine walked over to another cabinet by the makeup table and withdrew a leather bag from one of the drawers, then brought it back to the table. She reached into the bag and pulled out a cordless hair trimmer.

"Do you have a preference regarding your appearance?" she asked. "Do you prefer natural, neatly trimmed, or bare?"

I knew she was referring to my pubic hair, which I generally kept neatly trimmed. I'd always thought going fully bald was unnatural and unseemly, catering to men's prurient fantasies of fucking young schoolgirls. But in this situation, it seemed entirely appropriate, like I was stripping away all my camouflage and armor.

If tonight was all about being watched, I might as well bare myself in every sense of the word and truly let my inhibitions go. I began to fantasize about rubbing my bare pussy against Jasmine's while she poured warm oil between us. The more work she had to do on me, the more chance I'd have to make this last and hopefully get off.

I didn't hesitate. "Bare, thank you."

"As you wish," she said. "I'll remove the long hairs first with the trimmer, then shave you smooth with a razor."

No waxing? This was different. I was relieved to not have to bear the painful and violent trial of having my hairs ripped out en masse. Although shaving down there was always a scary proposition, I felt safe in the capable and practiced hands of this beautiful esthetician.

Jasmine nodded, then flipped a switch on the trimmer. The device buzzed softly as she placed it gently on my mound. I had only a light dusting of fur and it didn't take long for her to remove it with a few short strokes over my pubis. I shuddered as the vibrations penetrated deep into my core. If she had placed the flat head on my clitoris, I would have popped off in a millisecond. Instead, she turned the trimmer face-down and gently swiped the vibrating teeth against the sides of my vulva, sensuously separating my labia with her hands as she moved the device between my legs to trim the hairs on the inside and outside of my labia.

It was an insanely titillating feeling, but just clinical enough to bring me down from my plateau and shift my focus. My mind wandered to the upcoming feast, and I contemplated what surprises lay in wait at the main event. The hostesses had suggested there would be 'contact' of some sort during the meal, and I was intrigued exactly who and how it would be administered. The idea of being fully bald, cleansed, and thoroughly stimulated going into the event was an incredible rush.

Jasmine continued with the trimmer all the way down my perineum to my anus, barely touching me with the trimmer so as not to pinch any delicate tissues. Apparently there were no parts of my erogenous zone that would remain untouched, now—and perhaps later.

She turned off the trimmer and placed it at the foot of the table. Then she took a bottle of gel from the bag and spread the gel on her hands. Using both hands, she spread it gently between my legs, starting on my mound all the way down to my rosebud.

My body almost levitated above the table as Jasmine finally laid her hands directly on my clitoris. The gel had a mild stinging quality that added to the stimulating sensation. If this was meant to excite my follicles in preparation for the shave, it wasn't the only feature of my anatomy that it made erect. I could feel the hood of my clitoris retract as my button filled with blood and began to push outward. Suddenly, I was fully stimulated again and lusting for Jasmine's touch. I fantasized about her bending down and taking my swollen nub between her puffy lips and letting me come in her mouth.

Unfortunately, my satisfaction would have to wait a little longer. Instead, Jasmine reached into her bag and pulled out a straight-edge razor. In anyone else's hands, it might look threatening, especially in my prostrated and vulnerable position. But something about the way she delicately and sensuously opened the jackknifed tool instantly evaporated my fears. I could see how this type of razor would in fact give her better control safely cutting my stubs instead of the usual ladies plastic razor.

With her right hand, Jasmine gently laid the razor on its flat edge at the top of my mound, while she gently pulled my skin upwards with her other hand. Then she slowly turned the sharp edge perpendicular to my skin and began softly scraping the razor downwards. I could hear the bristling sound as the razor edge removed my nubs right down to the follicles. She repeated the pattern in one inch wide swipes on one side then the other of my pubis, being ever-so-careful to stop just where my clitoris lay quivering in a mixture of fear and excitement. There was something about the utter vulnerability of the procedure that made it the most erotic experience I'd ever had.

Jasmine used the same deft touch as she moved down my vulva and perineum, scraping the vestiges of stray hairs away with gentle swipes of the long blade, while sensuously separating my folds and flesh with her other hand. She took extra time and care around my anus and clit, using the gentlest and slowest motion I've ever felt someone apply to my body. The combination of fright and titillation as she probed my most sensitive body parts created a river of sensuous fluids running down my vulva. By this time, no shaving gel was necessary to provide a smooth gliding surface for the knife.

When she was finished, Jasmine retrieved a fresh wash towel from beside the sink and held it under the warm water faucet then twisted the excess water into the basin. She returned to the table and placed it over my splayed legs then gently cleansed the excess moisture and remaining shaving gel with gentle massaging movements of her hands. The warm, moist towel felt exquisite against my newly shaved skin. Jasmine's hands now felt comforting between my legs rather than erotic.

She had taken me on an incredibly sensuous erotic arc, right to the edge of ecstasy and back, to a quiet relaxed place. I exhaled fully and completely for the first time in almost an hour.

Jasmine removed the towel from between my legs and held up a large hand mirror at a forty-five degree angle toward me.

"What do you think?" she asked.

I tilted my head up and studied her masterpiece. Far from the usual red and swollen vulva that I typically experienced after the violent waxing with my regular esthetician, I'd never seen my pussy look so beautiful. Utterly bereft of any hair, my entire perineum from my pubic mound to my anus was totally bald, pink—and gorgeous. I just stared at my beautiful pussy, utterly transfixed by the transformation.

"You have to *feel* it to really appreciate how beautiful you are, Jade," Jasmine purred.

I moved my right hand down, running my fingers along the edges of my pussy. I gasped from a feeling I'd never felt before. It felt smooth as silk: no bumps or blemishes or cuts or bruises. It was almost as if I was feeling somebody else— somebody I'd never felt before. I couldn't stop my left hand joining the other in rubbing and caressing my sensitive organs.

Jasmine lowered the mirror and smiled at me as I felt the moisture begin to accumulate between my legs again.

"It's almost time for your dinner appointment," she said. "Why don't you save the best for last? I think you'll find plenty of ways to satisfy your appetite over the next couple of hours."

She lifted my kimono from the hook at the edge of the bathtub and held it open for me.

"I'll escort you downstairs now if you're ready. All you need to bring is your kimono and slippers—and your mask of course."

I sat up slowly and stepped off the massage table. Turning around, I held my arms out as Jasmine lifted one arm of the silk robe onto me then the other. Then she turned around to face me, wrapped the silk tie around me, and tied a single bow over my belly button. She retrieved my matching silk slippers and knelt down on one knee to gently lift my feet one at a time and place them softly inside. It took every ounce of my power not to grab her head and pull it into my pulsating pussy.

Jasmine stood up gracefully and smiled into my eyes.

"If you'll follow me, I'll escort you now to the fantasy feast."

She didn't bother putting her own robe on. Her tight little ass barely jiggled as she stepped smartly ahead of me. I wasn't sure if I'd have a chance to feel Jasmine's touch again before the evening was over, but for now I was in total bliss ogling her petite, curvaceous figure from behind...

Read More

www.facebook.com/authorvictoriarush
www.pinterest.com/authorvictoriarush
www.twitter.com/authorvictoriarush
authorvictoriarush@outlook.com

Hope to see you again soon!